TRAIL TO TOMORROW

a novel by Carrol Haushalter

To my friend mitchell

Happy Trails
Carrol Haushalter
Dec, 2010

Trail to Tomorrow

Library of Congress Control Number: 200990440

ISBN: 978-0-9814709-4-8

Printed in the United States of America

Boho Books paperback edition / June 2009

THIS STORY IS DEDICATED TO

All the girls with dreams of being a Cowgirl

Many thanks to all of those who helped to make this story possible:

To my husband, Pete, for his assistance, patience and understanding

To my daughter for her encouragement

To Lee Shaw for her advice and counsel

To the Molalla Writer's Group:

for their valuable feedback and encouragement.

CHAPTER ONE

Ma shuffled about our small one-room cabin as the smell of fresh brewed coffee filled the air. I should get up, but my bed was so warm and cozy, and the thought of my bare feet on the cold floor made me want to stay in bed.

Through the small window I saw daylight begin to peek along the edge of the dark blanketed sky while Ma continued her early morning coffee ritual. Quietly I watched as she sat at the table with her first cup. I think this is her favorite time of day. She slowly sipped away while gazing across the room as if in deep thought. I caught a swirl of gray in her hair from the glow of the oil lamp.

Ma has just about finished her cup of coffee. She'll be looking up to the loft where I sleep and giving me that "you better be getting up Allie Jo" look. Yeah, here it comes now. "I'm coming, Ma, I'll be just a minute."

I threw on my old cotton dress then brushed and quickly braided my hair. I straightened the blanket on my cot and tucked the sides under the feather mattress.

I share the loft with my two brothers. We hang up a blanket when they're home, so I can have some privacy. Right now they are away on a short cattle drive with Pa. Pa herds cattle to the market from places like Del Rio and San Antonio. My brothers are old enough to go with him, Joseph is eighteen and William is sixteen. I am the youngest at fourteen. Well, I will be in a couple of months.

I like it when the boys are home even though they tease me and pick on me unmercifully. Sometimes I wish I had a sister to talk and laugh with but my uncivilized brothers are all I have. We used to have a neighbor who had a daughter a year older than me, but they have since moved on. Neighbors out here are few and far between and the numbers keep dwindling.

I climbed down the ladder from the loft while Ma poured herself another cup of coffee.

"Morning Ma," I said as I slipped on my apron that hung by the door, and sat down on the bench to pull my shoes on. I loosely tied the laces because the shoes are beginning to get a little tight around my toes. I will be glad when summer is here and I can go barefoot. In the fall I will get a new pair. Ma will order them for me from the catalog at the mercantile.

I grabbed the pail and headed to our old drafty barn where our milk cow is stalled. We keep our livestock locked in the barn at night so the Comanches won't get them. They are bad about stealing folks' livestock. It's my job every morning to milk the cow and gather eggs from the hen house.

I pulled up the stool and positioned it close enough to do my job. The milk streamed out nicely as I worked one hand and then the other. She is the only cow we have. Ma calls her Sassy, but I don't know why, she is the gentlest cow I've ever seen. I don't mind milking her; I think we get along quite nicely.

After milking was done, I led Sassy out to a small pasture where she might find a little something to graze on. I also let my horse out to the pasture. He is an old paint named Tucker that Pa retired from the cattle drives when I was just a little girl. He is the only horse I have ever ridden and the only one that I ever want to ride. Pa and my brothers have their own horses and Ma doesn't ride, so Tucker is all mine. We are best friends and always will be; I don't care how old he gets.

Tucker lowered his head so I can wrap my arms around his neck and hug him while I run my hand down his mane. I squeezed his neck then gave him a kiss on his soft velvet nose before running back into the barn to fetch the morning milk.

I headed back with my pail of warm milk. Stopping at the hen house I gathered four brown eggs and stuffed them into my apron pockets. As I came from the hen house, I saw a sight that made me stop dead in my tracks. Not more than a few yards away, stood a coyote. I turned my head slowly from one side of the yard to the other to see if there were more. Coyotes usually run in packs at night, but strangely here he was in the morning sunlight. He snarled, showing his mouth full of sharp teeth. I slowly started inching my way back toward the hen house, where I could lock myself inside. The coyote lowered his head, but kept his dark eyes on me. White foam drooled from his mouth. He snarled again and staggered in my direction. My heart pounded in my throat and sweat started to form on my forehead. I wanted to yell for Ma, but I was afraid the beast would attack me if I made a sound. And I know that if I make a sudden move I will likely be his breakfast.

A blast echoed across the prairie that made me jump, sloshing the milk down my skirt and into my shoe. The coyote flew a good arm's length before dropping dead in the dry dirt. Ma stood in the doorway holding the long-gun, smoke oozing from the barrel.

"Althea Josephine! How many times must you be reminded to carry the gun? That could'a been a Comanche after the cow…. or you," she scolded. Ma leaned the long-gun against the door- frame and said, "We're gonna have to get rid of that rabid varmint. Give me the milk and eggs. I'll set them inside while you fetch a rope from the barn."

"Yes Ma." I said handing her the milk and eggs. My hands were shaking and my heart was still pounding from the scare. I hurried to the barn where we kept some rope, then met Ma back at the dead coyote.

We tied one end of the rope around the coyote's back legs, being careful not to get too close to his frothy mouth. We drug the critter a good ways downwind from the homestead until Ma felt we had gone a safe distance. I gathered sagebrush and dried cow dung and piled it all up in a heap while Ma went back to the cabin for lamp oil. We took the coyote by his back legs and lifted him onto the pile. I removed the rope and Ma poured some lamp oil to get the fire started. She lit the brush, letting the fire get off to a rip-roaring start before we headed back to the cabin. We had to burn the varmint so the rabies couldn't spread. If we just buried it, animals looking for food might dig it up, and we would have a big problem.

Back at the cabin we scrubbed up before Ma finished rolling out the biscuit dough. She makes wonderful biscuits and gravy. My biscuits are usually hard and the gravy is always lumpy. Ma says that I will never get me a husband if I don't learn to be a good cook, but I'm not too worried about getting a husband. If they are anything like my brothers, I don't think I want one.

Ma poured herself another cup of coffee before we sat to eat breakfast. She can drink more coffee than anyone I know. She's a little on the sickly side; Pa said she had a really rough time giving birth to me. He said I made her work real hard and just wore her out, so I do most of the hard chores around here while the men are gone. Cattle-drives can take two, three, and sometimes even four months. It gets really lonely around here while they're gone. Ma and I ate our breakfast in silence. Ma doesn't talk much. I think she wishes that Pa and my brothers were home too. Our spirits pick up when they're home. I must bore her terribly because I don't have the stories to tell that Pa does. Joseph and William also tell stories about happenings out on the trails that are exciting and sometimes funny. I wish I could be a cowboy.

I excused myself from the table to begin my daily chores. I picked up the water bucket from its place by the door before heading to the well.

The song of a whip-poor- will echoed around the nearby pecan trees as I lowered my bucket down the shaft. The crank squeaked as I pulled up the full bucket. I carried it back to the cabin, water sloshing out of the bucket all the way. Maybe it'll wash the milk out of my skirt.

Ma had an empty pan sitting on top of the still warm stove when I came back into the cabin. I poured some of the water into the pan. Ma took the bucket from me and said, "Allie Jo, I'll take care of the dishes if you'll run down to the spring house and fetch me the cream that I've saved from the last few milkings."

"Yes Ma'am." I said, and turned to go back out the door.

"Wait!" Ma said. "Take this with you." and handed me the fresh milk from this morning.

"Yes Ma'am." I took the milk and ran to the springhouse, careful not to drop the jar of milk.

The springhouse sat in a cluster of brushes beside the creek. It keeps the milk and cream cool. Ma had two jars of cream saved up. She usually doesn't save so much, but Pa and the boys will be home soon and she wants to be sure there is plenty of butter. Pa likes to slather butter thick on his biscuits and cornbread. It makes me sick to eat that much, but that's the way he likes it.

I hurried back to the cabin with the cream. Ma had just brought her butter churn out on the porch when I returned. She likes to sit in her chair and churn butter while she looks out across the prairie, probably watching for Pa.

"Ma, do you want me to go and hunt for rabbits now?" I asked, handing her the jars of cream. Pa taught me to hunt with the old long-gun so Ma and I can get fresh meat while he and the boys are gone. We had talked last night about getting a rabbit or two for supper. Ma thinks Pa and the boys will be home any day.

"Yes Allie, why don't you and when you get back I want you to build a campfire out there in the yard so we can cook stew for supper. It's such a nice warm day; I'd hate to heat the house up, if I don't have to.

Soon I was marching across the prairie carrying my gun and a few extra shells in my apron pocket. There is a cluster of old nut trees not too far away where rabbits have made a nest among the fallen limbs and branches. I would be able to find supper there. I would take Tucker with me, but I'm not going far and he's always been a little gun-shy.

I sat down at the bottom of a small tree with my back against its trunk, a little ways from the thicket. I waited with the long-gun laid across my lap. I waited and waited. The sun's warm rays beat down on me through the tree branches and began to make me drowsy.

My eyes popped open from what I hoped was just a short nap. Two turkeys stood at the opening in the brush. I can't believe it! We haven't had turkeys here in over a year. I can hear more of them in the thicket. Slowly, I took careful aim and squeezed the trigger. Feathers flew and all the turkeys scattered, except one nice big Tom. Good! I got one!

I hurried over to claim my kill, and watched the other turkeys quickly escape through the brush. I can't wait to show Ma what I have for supper *now!*

On the way home a warm breeze blew an awful smell my way that was oh-so-familiar. The musky odor of Javelina, *skunk pigs* is what we call them. There were five of the smelly creatures grazing through a patch of prickly pear cactus. Some folks, I'm told, have eaten the nasty things but not me. I hope I never get that hungry.

Quietly and quickly I headed for home, my shoes pinching at my toes.

Ma was sitting in her chair on the porch cutting up vegetables for the stew. "It's about time you showed up. You've been gone all morning."

"I'm sorry Ma," I said holding up my turkey, "But look at what I got!"

"Well," she said, "That'll do. He's a beauty."

I cleaned and dressed out the turkey and prepared it for the spit. I chopped some wood and started the cook-fire in the yard while Ma finished up the vegetables. I chopped more wood and stacked it near the fire so there would be a supply handy when we needed it.

After my wood chopping was done, I gathered the laundry Ma and I had hung out last evening. The sky had started to accumulate a few clouds as I finished up my outside chores for the day. I didn't have time to hoe the garden; that would have to wait until tomorrow. I milked the cow, then closed her up in the barn with Tucker for the night, before helping Ma carry the turkey into the cabin.

Pa, Joseph and William rode in just at dusk. Sprinkles of spring rain started to fall lightly onto the dry ground. Rain is always welcome around this part of the country. Kimble County can be awfully dry most of the year.

"Lawdy! What's been burnin' around here?" Pa asked, wrinkling his nose and reaching out to give Ma a hug and kiss.

"An old coyote," she said pushing herself away so I could have my turn.

"It was a rabid coyote and it almost got me," I interrupted as I got my hug.

"It almost got my girl?" Pa said patting my back.

"Yeah, I was almost a goner, but Ma shot it."

"Ma shot it?" he asked, raising an eyebrow.

"Joe, you gotta talk to that girl about carrying a gun." Ma said.

My brothers ran up after putting the horses up in the barn and tugged at my braids.

"Did ya miss us?" teased Joseph.

"Yeah, did ya miss us?" piped William.

"Yeah, like *typhoid!*" I said swatting at their hands.

"Hey! Settle down. Let's go inside, out of the rain, and eat. I'm starved," ordered Pa.

Ma's fresh roasted turkey sat on the stove waiting to be served. I had made the overcooked corn bread to be served with it.

We all sat down at the table for our evening meal. The boys ate like they hadn't eaten in a week.

"Where did this fine bird come from?" Pa asked. "It is certainly the best meal we've had in quite some time."

"Allie Jo shot it for yer supper, just this morning." Ma proudly replied.

"Then, why do I need to talk to her about guns, Elizabeth? Seems she knows what she's doin'." Pa joked.

"Joe, you are just hopeless to talk to!"

After a while the talk around the table became more serious.

"I'm tellin' ya Elizabeth, I don't know how we can make a livin' with the restrictions that is being put on the Longhorns. There's quarantine on cattle right now that's keepin' them from being sold to the markets back east. They're callin' it Texas fever. All because the eastern bred cattle are weak against the ticks that Texas long- horns carry. Ain't that sumpt'in, our livelihood dependent on a little ol' tick?"

My parents sat at the table after my brothers and I had gone to bed.

The oil lamp, with its low flame, showed just enough light for my parents to see each other's face.

They sat there talking quietly. I stretched my ears as far as I could; hoping to hear what they were talking about, but it was no use; the whispers were just too low.

CHAPTER TWO

Pa says there is a small cattle drive leaving San Angelo in a couple of weeks, going to Rio Hondo in the New Mexico Territory. Pa had talked to a trail boss named Ed Lewis. Mr. Lewis said we could join his drive if we meet them on the Concho River, just outside of San Angelo.

Moving is the only thing my parents can talk about. Pa says our lives will be better in the New Mexico Territory. Cattlemen, like John Chisum, are moving their whole spreads there and soon there won't be any herds left in West Texas. He says we have to go where he can make a living, and the cattle business is what he knows. I don't know how I feel about all this. I've never lived any place else, and to go with the cattle drive does sound awfully exciting. I can ride a horse as well as anybody and I can shoot a long-gun, too. Riding my horse, Tucker, and herding some cows across the country can't be all that difficult. Pa said I would be riding drag, which means I will be bringing up the rear. He also said I will have to carry my own weight, cause nobody will help me do my job. That shouldn't be too hard, nobody helps me do my job around here anyway, and believe me, nothin' is harder than chores.

Pa wants Ma and me to cut our hair short and dress like men. Pa doesn't know all the cowpunchers on the drive and isn't sure if they all can be trusted. He doesn't want outsiders to get wind that a couple of females are on the drive. It might be dangerous and it could complicate things for Mr. Lewis.

The next morning while I cleaned up the breakfast plates, Pa cut Ma's hair. I couldn't bear to watch. I busied myself with drying the dishes and cleaning, doing anything so I wouldn't have to look.

Pa's job was finally done and it was my turn. Tears welled up in Ma's eyes as she got up from the chair so I could sit. She went to the stove to pour herself a cup of coffee leaving her beautiful wavy hair lying on the floor. Ma looks much different than I expected her to and I suppose I will look much different too.

Pa cut and scrapped on my hair with his razor knife, yanking my head back with each scrape. Chills ran down my spine giving me goose bumps and I cringed as my hair fell to the floor. I don't know of any woman who has cut her hair off. Guilt crawled under my skin and I had the feeling that we were doing something sneaky and wrong. Finally the awful task was over. My fallen hair lay on the floor mingled with Ma's.

"Ok, girl, we're done," Pa said, patting my back, "Don't fret, it'll grow back before ya know it. Why don't ya go and try on them duds yer Ma has gathered for ya?"

"Yes Pa." I said brushing myself off before climbing up to the loft to change.

I sat on my bed and ran my fingers through what was left of my hair. A hot tear slowly made its way down my face. I pulled at the strands of hair and tried to stretch them in hopes of making them longer. It was, of course, no use. My once long dark hair now only reaches my ears. I liked being Pa's little girl, but that is all changing.

I felt ashamed, standing in the doorway wearing an old collarless cotton shirt and a leather vest that's a little big for me, and britches that William has outgrown. The britches, with buckskin sewn over the seat and down the inner thighs, felt strange when I walked. Pa says that I'll be glad of the buckskin after I've been in the saddle a while.

My worn out hand-me-down boots hardly had a heel left to walk on. The wide-brimmed hat came half way down over my ears, leaving me barely enough room to see. I snugged it down over my head as far as I could, and cautiously stepped into the early spring sunlight dressed in my new identity.

"Looka here, Will, its little Al all dressed in his new duds. Ain't he just adorable?" Joseph called out as he came from the barn.

"Why yes!" Will teased, "He's just a struttin' Rooster. Hey, little Al, let's see that new haircut of yers."

Heat built in my face as I tried to pull my hat down even farther. I turned to go back inside to keep from having to deal with these two heathens, but they were too fast. They quickly surrounded me and grabbed at my head, their hands tugging at my hat.

"Leave me alone!" I yelled holding tight to my hat.

"Aw, we just want to see yer haircut."

I kicked hard at William's shin as I tried to escape, causing me to fall to the ground and lose the grip on my hat. I rolled over and wrapped both my arms around Joseph's legs, bringing him down to my level. I squirmed around and was on top of him before he could react. He tried to block my fists by crossing his arms in front of his face. His laugh made my temper explode and caused me to lose all control of myself. My fists pounded at his face as I screamed in fury.

Something reached under my waist, pulling me off my brother and dragging me across the dirt. I was still swinging and screaming as I tried to get loose.

Suddenly I was plummeted into cold water, submerging me and filling my mouth and nose. I bounced back up, spitting and coughing. I sat in the watering trough as Pa stood there, his dark piercing eyes staring down at me. He then turned toward Joseph and William and said, "Must you boys tease your sister?"

"But Pa, we're just tuffinin' her up for the drive," explained William.

"You boys have been tuffinin' her up since she started walking! She is not some stray calf that we picked up along the trail. She is your sister. You are supposed to protect her, not torment her."

Pa took in a deep breath, looked down at me and turned back to the boys.

"I don't want to see any more of this!" he said as he walked away.

Pa seldom got mad, but I can always tell from his eyes when he's mad and this is one of those times.

I pulled myself up and stepped out of the watering trough. I shook myself like a dog, and tried to empty my soggy britches. Then I turned to go back inside the cabin to change my clothes.

Ma met me at the door. "You can change out back. I don't want those wet clothes in here," she said as she handed me my old dress.

"Yes Ma'am." I said and started to the back of the cabin.

"Althea!" Ma called.

I turned back. "Yes Ma?"

"You come see me when yer done dressing. I got a chore for you," she said, turning back into the cabin.

"Yes Ma'am." I answered. That's all I need is another chore, I thought, hoping Ma didn't notice the snip in my voice.

The dress was dry and cool in the warm spring air. A nice breeze blew across our small farm as I draped the wet clothing over the fence rails to dry before going to see what chore Ma had for me.

Inside the cabin, Ma was busy kneading bread dough.

"Ma, you got a chore for me?" I asked.

"I've already sent yer brothers out to finish picking the rest of those dried cowpeas. You get the wash tub ready for the harvest."

I carried Ma's washtub to a place that had a good breeze blowing through and sat it there. Joseph brought a sack of cowpeas from the field and left them with me. As he turned to go he said, almost under his breath, "I still think yer just adorable, Allie Jo."

I took the sack and rolled it with my hands to break up the shells. Then I emptied the sack into the washtub and stirred them around so the breeze could blow away the dry shells. When they were cleaned, I put the peas back into the burlap sack for storage.

* * *

It took a few days, but everything was finally neatly packed and tied down inside the wagon. There is not room for things like furniture but we did manage to load the cook stove. We could only take the most necessary things, food, cooking utensils, tools and our most precious personal items.

I had helped Ma load the inside of the wagon with three 25 pound bags of sugar, a large box of Ma's favorite Arbuckle's coffee, a couple tubs of molasses, the two sacks of cowpeas, baking soda, jugs of vinegar, two tubs of lard and all the jerky and canned goods Ma had left from the winter's storage supply.

My brothers strapped a barrel of flour and a barrel of cornmeal to one side of the wagon and they strapped a couple of barrels of water to the other side. There will be a chuck wagon on the trail for most of our eating during the move. This food is for when we get to our new home.

Pa tied our cow, Sassy, to the back of the wagon with a rope attached around her neck. He also attached a wooden coop to the side of the wagon that will carry our best laying hens and favorite rooster. Finally we are all packed and ready to go.

My bedroll was tied to the back of my saddle. The long-gun is tucked away in a scabbard that's strapped on the left side of the saddle and a lariat is tied on the right. I have to wear a pair of shotgun chaps that Joseph wore when he was thirteen. They are the climb-in type that nobody uses anymore. Cowboys now wear the bat wing style chaps. Strapped on my boots is a pair of work spurs with a gentle, star-shaped rowel. Tucker softly whinnied as I pulled myself up into the saddle. I know he is excited about our trip: he has been prancing around like a pony all morning.

We are on our way. The wagon rocked from side to side as we

made our way down the dusty road from our little cabin. I stopped to look back at our old home. My eyes welled up and a knot formed in my throat as it hit me. This is the only home I've ever known and most likely I will never see it again.

* * *

It took two days to reach the Concho River where we are supposed to meet the trail boss and the herd. I helped Ma set up the camp while the men took care of the livestock and refilled the water barrels. Ma got a fire started and set up the tri-pod to hang the cook pot while I gathered more firewood. She cut the meat for the stew while I pared the potatoes and carrots. I don't know why my brothers can't help. They're brushing down the horses; I don't think that is important right now. I wish I could go brush Tucker and lollygag around. You just wait; tomorrow I will be a cowboy too. Then I won't have to help Ma cook or do any "girl" chores.

After the supper dishes were cleaned and put away, I tucked myself into my bedroll beside the wagon. Even though I've been excited for days about this drive and the new home waiting for us in the New Mexico Territory, I understand there's no turning back and that scares me a little. The dark, wide-open prairie and the stars scattered across the night sky, made me feel small. I could hear my heart pounding in the night, as the moon's dim light slowly grew brighter.

Soon we will be joining a small cattle drive heading for the new territory and I will not only be dressed like a boy, I'll be acting like one as well. After living with my brothers, I figured I could manage it just fine. All I have to do is ride around on Tucker and gnaw on jerky.

I lay quietly listening to the coyotes calling out across the prairie with their yipping and yapping.

"Ya hear that Allie?"

My brother William scared me almost to death as he suddenly plopped down beside me.

"Will! Stop sneaking up on me!"

"Listen Allie," he whispered, "hear those coyotes? It could be Indians. Indians sound like that just before they sneak into a camp and steal little girls and take them back to their village and do - who knows what - with them."

"Stop it Will! I don't believe you!" I said, trying to sound brave.

"Well it's true, but don't worry, I won't let 'em git ya." He laughed as he jumped up and walked away.

Between my two brothers, Will teases me the most and I don't know if I should believe him or not, but just in case I'll scoot my bedroll and myself under the wagon. With Ma sleeping inside, I should be quite safe.

Just then a saddle dropped beside the wagon and in the moonlight Joseph rolled out his bedroll and crawled inside. He looked over at me and said softly, "Goodnight, Allie." Another saddle dropped and I quickly turned to the opposite side where Will was crawling into his bedroll. He, too, whispered, "Goodnight, Allie."

CHAPTER THREE

It was almost midday when the trail boss, Ed Lewis, rode into our camp. He and Pa talked a spell before joining the rest of us around the campfire.

Mr. Lewis told us about the events that happened on his way here. I sat deathly still, trying to hear every word. I held my knees to my chest and watched his thick red mustache flap up and down as he told about a run-in they had with some no-good rustlers.

"Yeah, it wasn't but a little ways from San Antonio," he said. "My boys were just too much fer 'em. Those crazy cowpunchers have fought off Indians up in the Comanche Territory; takin' care of a few rustlers was easy. They had those thieves hog-tied and strapped down on their horses ready for the Sheriff in no time. A couple of my men hauled them back to town."

Mr. Lewis then told a story about how Pa saved his red headed scalp. I was on my hands and knees trying to get as close as possible to hear it all. I settled in, sitting back on my heels.

"Back a few years ago," he started, "when we were just waddies, a small band of renegade Indians attacked the cattle drive. They were actually after the remuda."

"The fight was on," he continued, "arrows flew and guns blasted. The cattle were scattered all to hell and gone. An arrow shot through my shoulder just below the socket, knocking me from my horse. One of the red skins jumped off his horse and grabbed a handful of my hair with one hand and raised his knife with the other. I surely thought I was a goner. When your Pa blasted that savage with his pistol; he stopped his horse just long enough to pull me on behind. I rode on that horse's rump until it was safe to stop.

"Mr. Lewis," I asked, "How'd you get the arrow out of your shoulder? It must'a been painful."

"Oh" he said, "It was painful, but luck was on my side, the arrow went plumb through. The arrowhead was sticking out a couple of inches on the other side of my shoulder. Joe here, your Pa, broke off the arrowhead and yanked that arrow right out!"

"Wagon's coming!" Ma interrupted.

"Well, 'reckon we best go and meet Miguel. Ya know how he hates being ignored," said Mr. Lewis rising from the log he had been sitting on.

"Yeah, 'reckon we better," Pa joined in, stretching as he got up from his sitting place.

"Wait! What happened with the Indians?" I asked.

Joseph leaned over to me and whispered, "They're out there, Allie," motioning toward the open prairie. "They're watching and waiting until they can come and take yur scalp."

My hand slowly clutched dirt up off the ground, then quickly I threw it in Joseph's face. I shoved him backward onto his haunches as I stood up. I followed the rest of them to meet the new arrival.

A short stocky man jumped down from the wagon. He took off his sombrero and shook off the dust that had accumulated. Streaks of gray showed throughout his thick black hair. He climbed down from the wagon and shook hands with Pa and Mr. Lewis.

"Hola, Ed; Hola Jose, those beeves ain't far behind me. They be here soon," he greeted in broken English.

"Good to see ya, Miguel," Pa said. Pa turned around when I walked up, "Miguel, this is my youngest, Al, he's joined us on this trip."

"Hola, kid," said Miguel extending out his hand to shake mine.

"Hola," I said bashfully shaking his callused hand.

"Little Al, why don't you help Will unhitch Miguel's team?"

"Yes, Pa."

I helped Will, unhitch the two mules from the wagon. The men talked while we led the mules over to our team to be tied for the night.

The mule that I led stopped to show his stubbornness. I tugged hard on the lead rope, but the mule wouldn't budge. I dug my heels into the ground and pulled harder, "Come on you stubborn ol' mule!"

Will slapped the animal on his rump. It leaped forward, causing me to land on my rump. I quickly scrambled up and grabbed the rope and tied it with our livestock.

"There ain't no use talkin to that mule, unless yer gunna talk Mexican," said Will.

"Mexican?" I asked.

"Yeah, Miguel brought these mules from Mexico with him and he only speaks to 'em in Mexican, and he'll speak to us in Mexican, too— If he gets mad enough." Will chuckled.

"What do ya mean, if he gets mad enough?" I asked.

"I mean," Will continued, "When Miguel gets mad he forgets his English and starts spittin' out those Mexican words. You'll see soon enough. Come on, let's go." I finished brushing off the seat of my britches as I followed Will back to camp.

The chuck wagon was much different from our ordinary wagon. Miguel let down the hinged gate onto a swinging leg. It made a nice looking worktable. A large box, perched at the back of the wagon, had an assortment of different sized drawers and cubbyholes. A coffee grinder was attached to the side of the box and a large coffee pot sat on a shelf close by. In the boot beneath the box, the cooking utensils were kept. It was a real nice kitchen.

I peeked behind the box and saw bedrolls piled in a heap. There were also extra firearms. My mind raced, I wonder if the firearms are to fight off cattle rustlers or Indians?

"Hey, kid!" hollered Miguel.

Startled by his voice, I quickly jumped around to face him.

He tossed me a bucket and said, "Bring me water."

My heart pounded as I ran to the riverbank. I think I'll like being a cowboy.

CHAPTER FOUR

A cloud of dust was seen coming across the prairie. There! Coming from out of the dust are the beeves! Strung out for as far as the eye can see. Men were on each side of the herd, slowly moving the cattle. I ran out into open space for a better look. Pa joined me. He put his arm across my shoulders.

"What do you think about all those beeves?" He asked.

"I've never seen anything so magnificent!" I beamed.

"Look!" Pa pointed toward the herd. "Do ya see that group of horses beside those beeves?"

I squinted my eyes to get a better look. "I do see them, Pa."

"That's the remuda," he explained. "The extra horses are taken along on the drive so the men can have a fresh horse when they need one. Miguel's son, Antonio, is the wrangler out there. You won't see much of him; he will stay with the horses."

Soon the dust piled all around us as the men began to settle the herd down for the night just a little ways from camp. The men circled the cows until the tired beeves were all bedded down for the night. I'm use to Pa and my brothers being cowboys, but all these men are much different. They are not my family; they are *real cowboys!*

The cowboys straggled into camp one and two at a time. A lot of them didn't seem to be much older than Joseph. They tied their horses with ours, before pulling their saddles off the tired animals and dropping them down on whatever spot they claimed for their own. Then they got in line for their supper. I took my place at the end of the line. I got a big whiff of bad smelling body odor. It was almost too much to handle, but I'm sure I'll get use to it.

Miguel said we're going to have Pecos strawberries for supper. I can hardly wait! I love strawberries and I never dreamed we would have them with our meal.

I sat down on the ground crossed legged to eat my supper. I dug my spoon around in my food, trying to find the strawberries. I think Miguel made a mistake. Supper is nothing more than beans and biscuits.

Pa came and sat down beside me. He spoke to me quietly, "Yer Little Al now, a waddie on this drive. Watch these men, the way they eat and the way they walk. You will have to copy them in some of their cowboy ways. What I'm saying is; try to fit in and be one of the boys where you can and stay close to your brothers or me, when you can."

"Yes sir, Pa, I'll try. But I have a question."

Pa turned his head toward me, "What's on yer mind?"

"Well, Miguel said we were having Pecos strawberries for supper and all I have are these red beans. Do you think he forgot?"

Pa's face went blank. Then he looked puzzled. "Lawdy, Allie Jo, You are a greenhorn. Those red beans are called Pecos strawberries and that biscuit yur eaten is a sourdough bullet." He smiled and shook his head. "I'll be keeping my eye on you, but for now yer gonna have to lose some of those manners that yer Ma has taught you. I draw the line on cussin'. That's one thing you ain't gonna do."

He patted my knee and went to join the others around the cook pot. I looked around at the men eating. Most of them ate with their hand over top the spoon handle, using it like a shovel, so I did too. I used my shirtsleeve for my napkin. I sure hope Ma accepts my manner- less ways.

Soon the men had finished eating. Some squatted in a group and traded stories. Others rolled cigarettes and smoked while they rested.

"Hey Sam!" someone called out, "when you gonna tell me about that girl up in the Brazos?"

Sam's face looked like dark leather, showing his years of riding in the sun. His brown hair hung almost to his shoulders under his wide-brimmed hat. Pistols, strapped in their holsters, hung on each hip.

"Oh yeah, Jake. Come on over here and I'll tell ya now," he said.

He then told Jake about some ol' whore that lived in a town that I never heard of.

Jake's rotten teeth showed when he spit tobacco out between the gap he had from a missing tooth. His oily dark hair curled around his ears. He gave a laugh that made my stomach quiver. Sam talked more about that whore. I don't think I should be listening to them talk that way.

There was a man lying on the ground on his bedroll, his head resting on his saddle, smoking a cigarette. Red hair poked out from under the hat that he was still wearing. He was quiet and didn't seem to be bothered with all the chatter that was about. As I watched him, he slowly turned his head toward me and our eyes met. I wanted to look away but that's when I saw the ugly scar that ran the length of his cheek. A shiver ran down my spine. One side of his mouth curled up in a grin or a sneer, I'm not sure which, before he turned his gaze and snubbed out his cigarette.

The clickity clack of horse hooves shifted my attention to a young rider who came from the first watch with the cattle. His tall, slender body slid from his horse. Blonde hair hung to his shoulders from under a weather beaten hat. A holstered pistol sat on the front of his left hip. A large knife, snug in a sheath, was attached low on his leg. The sheath seemed to be part of his tall moccasin boot. He dressed differently than all the other men; he wasn't even wearing a shirt.

His steps were quick and quiet as he walked in my direction. He didn't walk with the same rolling amble as the other cowboys. His face was handsome, more than any of the rest I'd seen. He looked down at me as he passed by. I quickly dropped my eyes down to my supper and ate like it was my only meal this week, but I watched him from the corner of my eye as he walked to the chuck wagon. He took a plate of beans and a biscuit from Miguel, and sat at the bottom of a nearby tree.

"Hey Little Al," said Will, squatting down beside me. "I seen ya eye-ballin that half-naked man over there," nodding toward the stranger.

"I was not! And you need to stop sneakin' up on me," I demanded.

"I'm not sneakin. You have to be more aware of yur surroundings. Out here in the open range someone is likely to come up behind ya and slit yer throat! Maybe even that almost Injun over there," he said motioning toward the man.

Will then slapped me between my shoulders, nearly causing me to spill my beans. "But don't ya worry. I'm watchin you."

My brother walked over to his horse to take his turn with the cattle.

"I'm not a baby, I'm a cowboy," I muttered to myself.

I glanced back to where the stranger was, and then quickly looked all around. Where did he go?

After supper I crawled into my bedroll under our wagon. My stomach felt full of butterflies. I lay on my side and gazed out into the darkening prairie. A small fire flickered all alone out in the distance. I watched it until my eyes were too heavy to stay open.

CHAPTER FIVE

Dawn came just a comin' when I crawled out from under the wagon. After rolling up my bed, I grabbed a bucket and the small milking stool from the back of the wagon. Walking over to where Sassy was tied, I sat down on the stool and began milking. The sun hadn't even peaked over the horizon yet, but I was soon done and delivered the bucket to Ma.

The men rolled up their bedrolls and tossed them into the chuck wagon, so I did too. I got in line behind the last man, who was the red haired man with the ugly scar on his face.

Ma passed out her wonderful biscuits topped with a dab of honey. She gave a low grunt as she handed each man their breakfast. When it came my turn, she grabbed my hand and patted it. She smiled from under her hat brim as she handed me my biscuit, before motioning me away.

I didn't know what to do, so I saddled Tucker, and climbed up on his back to wait for Pa. Everyone was putting the cattle back into single file. Ma and Miguel were busy packing up their gear. Ma seemed to work well with Miguel. I wonder if he knows that she's a woman.

The camp was mostly cleared-out now. I wish I knew what to do. I feel like such a knot-on-a-log.

Thank goodness, Pa finally rode up. "Good to see yer ready fer work," he said. "Come on and I'll introduce ya to yer partner."

"Yes sir, Pa." I gently tapped my spurs against Tucker and followed him.

We went the opposite direction that everyone else had gone. Tucker nickered and seemed to strut a little more than usual. He seems excited about being with so many cattle and other horses. I don't think he misses the farm at all. We rode all the way to the back of the herd where an older man was sitting in his saddle with his right leg hooked around the saddle-horn. He was tall with hardly any meat on his bones. His horse was a gelding that looked much younger than Tucker.

Pa said, "Hey, Lum."

"Hey, Joe," he softly answered back.

Pa introduced me, "This is my youngest, Little Al. He's gonna ride drag with you on this trip. I want you to teach him what he needs to know and see to it that he keeps out of trouble."

"Yes, sir, I will surely do that, Joe. Don't you worry," said Lum.

Pa turned his horse to leave. He looked back at me and said, "You do as Mr. Columbus tells you and you'll do just fine."

I nodded. Pa clicked his heels to his horse and rode away. I looked back at Mr. Columbus. I was awful nervous. I've never been on my own before.

"Come on, Little Al, we got work to do." He said as he smiled and ran his fingers across one side of his mustache and curled up the tip. His narrow face made his mustache look huge.

"Yes, sir, Mr. Columbus." I said, as manly as I could.

"Ahh, you don't have to be all formal. Most people just call me Lum," he said.

"Yes sir, Lum. And you don't have to call me 'Little Al'. You can call me just Al." I said as grown up as I could muster.

"Ok, Just Al," he said.

"No, no, just call me Al," I explained.

"All righty then, Al," he smiled. "Let's get to work."

The main body of the herd trailed along behind the leaders, guarded by outriders known as swing. They saw to it that none of the herd strayed or dropped out. The cattle moved slow and of their own free will. There's no driving to do. Lum said to never let a cow take a step, except in the direction of its destination. It's good for the condition of the herd to keep them calm and relaxed and to move them slowly. Lum says that makes the days very tiring and extremely long.

There was nothing for miles, just sagebrush and chollo cactus. Lum didn't talk much; he mostly stayed pretty quiet. He sat with that one leg hooked around the saddle horn all day just moseying along. For him to answer a question sometimes took awhile. At first, I thought he didn't hear me, then out-of-the-blue, he would start answering a question that I'd done forgot I asked.

I asked him about some of the men. Where did they come from? Did they have families?

"Well, there's Jake," he said. "He's just plumb rotten to the core, but he's good with cows. He's known for getting drunk and rowdy."

"Even here when he's working on a cattle drive?" I asked.

"Yeah," he said, slowly looking over the cattle. "You might try and avoid him whenever possible. He ain't got no respect for women or kids, that's fer sure."

"Yes sir, I will," I assured him.

"Now, if you look at Frank, he's got a wife and a houseful of young'uns back in San Antonio. During the winter months, he stays home and works with his father-in-law at the livery stable."

"Then there's Levi, I don't know much about that red headed scar face. He's fairly new with this outfit."

"What about you, Lum? What's yer story?" I asked, swinging my leg around my saddle horn, like him.

"Aw, I ain't got no family. I'm just an ol' saddle-stiff," he said swiping a fly from his face.

He didn't look like a man who spent his whole life in a saddle.

"Aw," I said swatting my hand at him, "you ain't no saddle-stiff."

He looked at me most seriously. "Yeah, I am."

I stared ahead for a few minutes, not wanting to carry that conversation any farther. "What about the young man with the moccasin boots?" I finally asked.

"That's Cole Howard," he said. "He's truly done lived a sad story." Then he pointed to a calf that had just lain down in the grass. "Why don't you go put that calf back with its Mama?

"Yes sir." I said and went off to get the calf. It's my job to make sure that no calves are left behind.

"Come on, little feller, lets go join yer mama." Although the calf jumped up from the nudge of Tucker's nose, it just stood there not making another move. Swinging off my horse, I took the calf's tail and pulled it up over its back until it was trotting toward the herd. I climbed back up into the saddle and moved in behind the dawdling calf. Tucker, being an experienced cattle horse, put his head down and gently bit the calf's rump. It finally ran to its mother and I hurried back to Lum to hear the sad story.

"Well," Lum leaned on his saddle horn with both hands, to stand in his stirrups, "Looks like we'll be having our noon meal just a little early today. The boys have started to settle the herd down up ahead."

"Oh good," I said, "That biscuit didn't last me very long."

The jerky from my pack helped tide me over, but it's not like a real meal. I was getting real hungry. When Lum and I got to the chuck wagon, there wasn't much food left. The men had rotated around to watch the herd while others ate.

The noon meal was a flour tortilla filled with the left over Pecos strawberries. I was given two helpings, which I wolfed down and followed it with a cup of water from the drinking barrel. During the break, some of the men took naps. I did too.

Ma and Miguel started out ahead with the wagons, before we stirred the cattle, so they could set up evening camp and have supper ready by the time we arrived.

I had just pulled myself up in my saddle when Cole rode by. His blonde hair flowed in the breeze when he took his hat off to beat the dust from his chaps. He doesn't look any worse for wear and I wonder what kind of sad story he lived? Maybe he was robbed and the bandits took his clothes. I'll have to remind Lum. He probably forgot that he was going to tell me the story.

Will rode up, blocking my view of Cole.

"Tsk, tsk, tsk" he said, shaking his head, then rode off behind Cole. I glared after him in disgust. His teasing has always infuriated me.

I joined Lum at our spot at the back of the line hoping he would finish his story about Cole. I found that I wasn't quite brave enough to ask again. I didn't want him to get the idea that I was interested, which I'm not. I'm a boy. A cowboy.

Things were pretty quiet as we loafed along. We didn't talk much. My mind wandered back to our old home in Kimble County. I wonder if varmints have invaded the cabin. I thought about Mr. and Mrs. O' Bryan who owned the mercantile in town, especially Mrs. O'Bryan. Mr. O'Bryan was very stern and grumpy most of the time, except when Pa was with Ma and me. He was always real nice to Pa. Mrs. O' Bryan was nice all the time. She had curly red hair and a smiley round face sprinkled with freckles. She always gave me a penny candy whenever I came into the store. Mr. O'Brien would scoff at it, but Mrs. O'Brien would pat my hand and say, "Don't pay any attention to him, dear, he's all bark and no bite." Then she would smile so sweetly at him and he would walk away. I can still see her cheerful smile.

"Yeah, yeah." Lum shook his head, "Pretty sad indeed."

"What's sad?" I asked, coming back.

"Why, Cole, of course. Isn't that who we were talkin' about?" he asked.

"Oh, yes, of course." He now had my attention.

" He's as nice a feller as you'd want to meet," he continued. "When he was just a little boy, maybe about five, a band of renegade

Indians raided his family's farm and rode off with him. I heard it was some time before they got the boy back."

"How long did the Indians keep him?" I asked, glued to his every word.

"Oh, I think about 7 or 8 years. He never went back to the white man ways and he was unable to go back to his Indian family. At night you can see his campfire in the distance. He likes to camp alone. He started working cattle drives when he was just 14 years old."

"That's how old I am!" I boasted.

That was all of our conversation for the day. Lum took more interest in the cows now, so I did too, but I couldn't get my mind off of that poor little boy, stolen away from his family.

CHAPTER SIX

After supper, some of the men rolled themselves a cigarette and laid back to enjoy their smoke. Lum and I sat by the campfire and listened to Frank pick a little on his guitar. The moon's light was glowing brightly at half full. My brother, Joseph, wearing the look of concern on his face, asked "Has anyone heard about a family that had been attacked by injuns last fall?"

"Nah, don't believe I have." said Will.

"Oh yeah," recalled Frank, "I think I heard about that. Didn't they kill that farmer and then take his wife and children hostage?"

"Yeah, that's what I heard. Don't know if they ever rescued that woman and her young'uns." said Joseph.

"Well, that's just a shame," said Will. "I bet they were a nice family too."

"What do you think happened to those children and their ma?" I asked.

"Well, Little Al," said Frank, "I hate to say, but they probably made slaves out of them, or they could have scalped them, or maybe they just ate them for supper. Who knows what those savages done to those poor folks?"

Joseph interrupted, "Come on, Little Al, it's our turn with the herd."

My brother and I fetched our horses and rode out to where the cattle were bedded down. We relieved Pa and Cole. They each nodded their departure before riding off toward camp for their meal and rest. Cole wore a Mexican poncho over his shoulders. I guess he does wear clothing occasionally.

Slowly riding Tucker in circles around the sleeping herd, I couldn't get that woman and her children out of my mind. I tried to make sense of it all. Back home in Kimble County, Indians didn't scalp anybody. All they ever did was steal livestock. They didn't steal people, at least not anymore. I've heard stories of such happenings, but that was back in the olden days. That kind of thing is unheard of in this day and time. These northern Indians must be quite different and awfully uncivilized.

Across the circle of cattle, I heard Joseph sing a sweet lullaby. He has always had a nice singing voice. My family says that I sing like a screaming eagle. Ma said that Joseph got his singing voice from Grandma Meeks, and that I got Grandma's temper. It just doesn't seem right.

The following morning we had a very nice breakfast with salt pork, pickled eggs and biscuits. I had just handed my empty plate to Miguel when Joseph called to me, "Hey Little Al! Why don't 'cha come and sing these cows awake for us this mornin'?"

"What do you mean?" I innocently asked.

"You know," he said, "You can scare them awake with yur eagle screamin."

The men all laughed. I was overcome with embarrassment. Then my face blistered with rage. I will *kill* that heathen. Like a bolt, I tackled my brother, my fists swinging wildly. I was out for *blood*! He will never embarrass me like that again! I felt stinging across my backside, but I wasn't giving up until he had reaped my wrath!

Joseph managed to push me off. He jumped up and ran for his horse.

"There's more of that fer ya, Joseph Raymond, if ya mess with me again!" I yelled.

Ma always calls out our middle names when she's mad, so I couldn't help but do the same. I picked up my hat and dusted myself off. I thought to myself that I had done a good job of showing him. Then I turned and found Ma standing there with her arms crossed and holding a long-handled wooden spoon. Now I know what the stinging was. Her face was stern and her eyes dark. If looks could kill, I'd been dead just sure as the world.

I took a step back, turned on my heels and ran! I didn't know that I could saddle a horse and be gone as fast as I do now. I headed after my brother in a dead run. I guess I could wake the cows, just this once.

CHAPTER SEVEN

We finished supper and settled into our usual evening routine. Pa and Will were taking the first watch with the cattle. Carrying a bucket in each hand, Ma headed to the river to fetch water to clean the dishes. After a little bit, I followed Ma to the river hoping she could stand watch while I relieved myself.

Humming, as I hurried along, I heard voices down at the river. I looked toward the water and saw someone with Ma. I can't quite make out who it is. Ma's voice got louder. I hurried faster, straining my eyes to see. He pulled Ma close to him. She cried out as she struggled to get free.

I broke into a full run. It was Jake! And he's trying to kiss Ma!

"Stop!" I hollered racing toward them.

They tumbled to the ground with Jake landing on top.

I threw myself on Jake and pounded him with my fists. He shoved me off. I kicked him in the side with all my might. He let out a loud moan as I swung my leg to kick him again. He grabbed my boot and flipped me to the ground. I scrambled up to get another kick in, when his fist hit my face. Back down I went, my nose throbbing in pain. He reached down and got a hand full of my shirt. Yanking me up, he punched me, again. I could barely hear Ma screaming as she tried to pull Jake away from me. My ears rang and my face was numb.

Jake broke from his hold and I fell to my knees with the world spinning. Ma knelt beside me as I tried to gather my wits. She cradled me in her arms, sobbing.

Then she screamed, "Joseph! Stop!"

I lifted my head and saw my brother Joseph beating the tar out of Jake. He was like a mad man. It looked like he would kill Jake with his bare hands. The trail boss and the cowboys from camp, had all come running to see what trouble had brewed. Levi and Frank pulled Joseph off of Jake and held my brother by his arms as they tried to get him to settle down.

"What's going on here?" demanded Mr. Lewis.

"We got us a woman on this drive!" said Jake, spitting blood from his mouth and pointing at Ma.

"Yeah, I know," said Mr. Lewis. "Her name is Elizabeth. She's Joe's wife. She tried to pass herself off as a man so there wouldn't be any trouble from snakes like you."

"Aw, hell, Boss! You shoulda known better than to bring a woman along. You musta known there'd be trouble."

Joseph made another move at Jake, but the two men kept their hold.

The trail boss walked over to Jake and took a big sniff. "You been drinking again, Jake. Every time you get to drinking, you cause me some kind of trouble. I can't take anymore from you so you pack up, and git out now. If you're smart, you'll be gone before Joe finds out that you tried to have your way with his wife."

When Jake headed back toward the camp, Levi and Frank let go of Joseph. Mr. Lewis turned and walked back to where Ma and I stood, "Come on Elizabeth, I'll walk you back to camp."

"No. I have to help my ...."

My brother interrupted, "It's OK, Ma, I'll get him cleaned up for ya." He put his hand on my shoulder.

"Let Joseph take care of Little Al, Elizabeth, and you come with the rest of us. I'll send Cole out to relieve Joe for you."

I hadn't noticed how much blood was on my face and shirt. My nose is still slowly trickling and I think there is a cut over my eye. Joseph took my neckerchief and wet it in the cool water. I could feel the soreness in my face as my brother washed it and I winced at his touch.

"Looks like yer workin up a good shiner, Allie Jo." Joseph said and started to chuckle.

"What's so dang funny?" I asked.

"Ah, I was just thinkin. When Will finds out about this, he'll be fit to be tied."

"What do you mean?" I asked, still puzzled.

He laughed and said, "Well, here you and me are in this big brawl and Will missed out."

I laughed a little, "Oh yeah, he would of surely wanted in on it."

Still laughing, Joseph said, "And not only that, but when Ma gets her senses back and realizes that we've been fightin', why, she'll probably whoop us both with that wooden spoon of hers."

He busted out laughing and so did I.

CHAPTER EIGHT

The sun was just peaking over the horizon, but the throbbing in my face had already awakened me. Miguel had a shaving mirror hanging on the back corner of the chuck wagon, so I peeked and immediately wished I hadn't. I was an awful sight. My eye, swollen almost shut, was a shiny black and blue color. My nose is puffy and purple. Ma didn't say anything to me. She just touched my face and gave a half-hearted smile. My brothers have always scuffled with me. I've kicked and hit them quite often in my lifetime, but neither one has ever hit me back. I'm sure glad of that. Jake would probably have beaten me to death, if Joseph hadn't come to my rescue. Ma was no match for the likes of Jake. For that matter, neither was I.

Everyone had started moving about in the usual morning routine. Thank goodness Jake had cleared out before Pa came in from the night watch. Will was still asleep in his bedroll, his hat lying over his face. Most cowboys sleep with their hats on, I guess so they don't misplace them.

"Hey! Will! Get up lazy bones." Playfully, I yanked the hat away. Sweat covered his pale face. His eyes were wide and fixed and they didn't even blink.

Slowly I leaned over my brother and whispered, "Will?"

The soft rattle of a snake came from his bedroll. Quietly I stepped back.

"What's wrong?" a voice from behind me asked.

"Shhh," putting my hand out to stop the cowboy. I turned slightly to see Cole standing there holding a gnawed piece of jerky. "There's a rattler in my brother's bed."

He stuffed the jerky in his vest pocket and dropped down to sit on his heels. He listened quietly, and then motioned me to move back farther.

"What are we gonna do?" I whispered while stepping back.

Ignoring me, Cole inched closer to Will. He spoke low. "Will, I'm gonna grab the snake. When I say, *now*, you roll out as fast as you can, ok?"

Will blinked in response. My trembling kept me from moving away any farther. Never before have I seen such fear in a person's face.

"*NOW,*" Cole yanked the bedroll as Will quickly rolled across the dirt then scrambled to his feet. Cole threw down the bed and waited like an animal on a hunt, ready to pounce on its victim. The snake slithered from the pile of bedding. In one smooth motion, Cole grabbed the snake's tail, whirled it around his head once then cracked it like a bullwhip. The head snapped off and landed at my feet.

"What are you boys doing? Playing around? We got cows to push, let's get a move on."

I whirled around, "Pa! A rattler was in Will's bedroll, with Will still in it!"

"What? A rattler?" asked Pa as he eyed the snake that dangled from Cole's hand.

"Yeah, Cole yanked it away from Will, then snapped its head plumb off!"

"Well," said Pa, "It's a wonder ya'll didn't scream like little girls."

"But Pa, you should'a seen it happen, and Will was scared almost to death!"

"Well, it's all over now, Little Al. We need to get a move on and get these beeves moving." Leading his horse away, Pa walked back toward the chuck wagon. Maybe he'll tell Ma. Will didn't say anything. He just stood there looking down at his bedroll scattered in the dirt.

Cole swung the decapitated snake over his shoulder and started to walk toward the wagon. "I think I'll take this to Miguel. Maybe he will fix it for my noon meal." He looked back at my still pale brother and smiled. "Maybe I'll share it with you, Will. After all you found it."

Cole gave a little laugh and went on his way carrying the snake that could have been the death of my brother.

"Will, do you want me to help you with your bedroll? I asked, making a move.

"No, It's okay, I got it. We better get to work," he said.

CHAPTER NINE

Most days were long, hot and tiring. We would walk along side of our horse for a good stretch at a time, just for some kind of exercise. Other days we found ourselves counting the horns of dusty ol' cows.

I would find myself thinking about the loft in our tiny cabin. I sometimes miss waking up to the smell of Ma's Arbuckle Coffee. I used to watch the horizon for Pa and my brothers, hoping to see them coming home after delivering cattle to Kansas or some other destination. Life sure can change.

Lum and I have become good friends. He says the New Mexico Territory is more exciting than Texas. I can hardly wait to see for myself.

The dry grass crackled as a breeze shook their blades. A low whistling sound began to echo across the prairie. It had an eerie sound that gave me a shiver.

A flash suddenly streaked across the blue gray sky.

"Ya better be on yer toes, Al. This might be bad." Lum said, his eyes sweeping over the cattle.

I, too, began to look for signs of stress in the cattle. A couple more bolts flashed. The cattle flinched as they marched forward. Lum and I untied our slickers from our packs and slipped them on. We prepared best we could for what could come our way.

Joseph galloped up, his horse's hoofs kicking into the dirt causing the dust to rise in a cloud. "Hey, Little Al. Pa wants you to git to the wagon. You got to hang onto Sassy so she doesn't spook and get tangled up with these cattle. Hurry! You ain't got time to lollygag."

He spurred his horse and rode off into the herd.

"You best hurry, Al. You got to take care of that milk cow," Lum said, nodding toward the wagons.

I raced to the wagon and climbed inside the back end. I tied Tucker next to Sassy. The wagon rocked as Ma slapped the horses' necks with the reins while I hung onto Sassy's rope. I could see white in the cattle's eyes as they began to mill in closer and closer to each other. When the roar of the storm set in, the herd went into a full-blown stampede.

Rain poured from the sky and water danced on the dry ground. The wagon was swaying hard as Ma tried her best to keep the team under control. The men were working hard to try to turn the herd, trying to force them to circle. Sassy flung her head up, squirming to get away. My hands ached from the burn of the rope, but I held tight.

Finally the cattle began to circle, slowing their pace. The storm blew on as fast as it had come in. Ma pulled the wagon to a stop. When she got down and came back to soothe Sassy, I climbed back onto Tucker and rode out to help look for runaway strays.

A horse nickered from behind. I turned Tucker around expecting to see Lum, but there were two Indians instead. One quickly grabbed my bridle. I kicked Tucker hard and he reared as I tried to escape.

"You ain't gonna scalp me!" I yelled, striking at them with my reins while kicking my horse. I was reaching for my gun when another hand stopped me.

"Settle down, they won't hurt you," a voice said. Cole lifted his hand from mine and he then spoke to the Indians in their own language. They seemed to argue somewhat. Cole then told Lum to ride out and rope a steer and bring it back. The Indians let go of my horse. Lum quickly returned with a steer and he handed it over to one of the Indians. Cole reached over and grabbed Tucker's bridle, pulling me away. When the three of us were far enough away, I asked Cole, "What did you say to them?"

"I told them that you were my kin."

I felt my face flush as I asked, "That I am your kin?"

"Yeah, I told them that you were my kid brother."

"Oh", I stammered, "That was good thinking."

"They didn't really want you, anyway, they were hungry and only wanted some beef."

CHAPTER TEN

The days have been getting much hotter since the thunderstorm, hotter than any we've had since the beginning of the drive. The sun's fierce rays beat down on us mercilessly. It's our third day without water for the beeves and we are all more sparing with our own water. There is no wind or even a breeze to cool our bodies. Sweat drips down my back. My feet, sweating inside my boots, began to itch. The dust hangs thick in the air; I can almost see it puff from my mouth, when I cough. The beeves are exhausted from the heat and the lack of water. I've been praying constantly for a watering hole. Texas gets awfully hot during the summer, but I don't recall it ever getting *this hot*.

Lum and I walked beside our horses for long stretches at a time to keep them from over-heating. The other men did the same. Walking helped my itchy feet, but my pinkies were getting blistered from rubbing the inside of my boots.

Tucker suddenly yanked his head up. His ears pointed upward and his nostrils flared. I held the reins tight as my horse pulled like he wanted to take off running. Lum's horse did the same. The cows bawling became louder. Their horns clashed and they picked up speed.

"Lum! What's gotten into them?" I asked.

"Hallelujah!" he yelled, climbing up on his horse. "They smell *water*! You better mount up!" He said reaching over to hold Tucker's bridle, keeping him steady as I climbed up. "Be on yer toes, Al, they might run."

And run they did, across the mesa and down the slope to the Pecos River.

Lum and I stopped at the mesa's edge. We looked down at the

cattle and the river. Its twists and turns made a shape that looked like a horse head. I'd heard stories of the infamous Horse Head Crossing. It's tricky to cross the river because of the quicksand traps hiding in the river's bottom. The channel changes frequently, making it hard to find safe footing. Horse Head Crossing is well known for its killing ways.

"Well, just looka there." Lum said shaking his head in disbelief. "Those dumb cows ran plumb across the river.

"Why did they do that?" I asked, hardly believing it myself.

"Oh, they just got in a big hurry I guess. We'll be setting up camp on the other side of the river fer the night so the beeves and horses can all get their bellies full of water before we head up into the New Mexico Territory.

Lum and I slowly made our way down to the river. Skeletons laid along the banks. Cow horns can be seen, just under the water, at the river's edge.

"Come on Little Al. Stay close to me and cross where I cross. I want you in my sight just in case we have trouble," Lum instructed.

"Yes sir, I will." I answered as we slowly started down the embankment into the river.

I was staring at Lum's back, just before stepping into the river, when something caught my eye. Someone was plunging back into the river from the other side.

Cole was headed toward a calf that was having trouble crossing the water. He threw his lariat and roped the calf, I saw him tug on his rope, then slide off his horse. Oh no! It looks like he's in trouble.

"Lum! It's Cole and he's in trouble! I'm goin' to help!" I yelled, then spurred Tucker and turned him to run up the bank, then into the river toward Cole.

"No! Al! Cole doesn't need yer help!" Lum yelled, but it was too late, for I knew Cole was in trouble and I had to hurry. After all, didn't he help me when I was in trouble with the Indians?

Suddenly, Tucker stumbled. He whinnied and lunged forward, then lunged again. I tapped my spurs into his sides to encourage him to move forward. He reared up kicking his front legs above the water, throwing me from his back. The cold water swallowed me. I quickly lost my sense of direction and found myself grabbing the bone of a skeleton trapped in the mud under the murky water. My heart jumped into my throat and in a panic I tried to swim to the top of the water but my boots held me in the mud. I struggled to free myself, but the only way I could get loose was to slide out of the boots. I screamed as soon as I felt air. I reached out to

Tucker and grabbed a stirrup. His eyes bulged and he too was screaming in terror.

"*Quicksand*!" I screamed. "*Help*!"

I could hear Lum's voice above the rushing of the water.

"*Lum*!" I yelled. I could see him take the rope from his saddle.

"Hang on, Tucker. Help's cummin." I said to my horse. The panic in me wasn't helping him much. He was fighting quicksand, struggling against the river. It was taking all I had to hang on. The current was dragging at my legs, pulling me away. My hands were getting numb from the cold water, making it hard to hang on to the wet leather.

"God please don't let us die, I prayed."

A rope landed up stream floating towards me.

"Al! Put the rope under yer arms and hang on to it," came Lum's instructions.

One arm and then the other, I placed through the noose in the rope, but I continued to barely hang onto the stirrup.

"Let go of the horse!" Lum yelled.

"No! I can't leave him here!"

"*LET GO OF THE HORSE!*" he commanded.

The rope jerked my body. I had no choice but to let go. I grabbed the rope with both hands. Water stung my face as Lum pulled me with his horse to safety. Cole ran into the water and helped me onto the bank. He turned me over on my stomach and pushed down on my back as I coughed and spit water from my mouth. Next thing I knew, Pa was kneeling beside me.

"You all right, Little Al?" Pa asked as he helped me to sit up.

I coughed a few more times while Pa patted my back.

I coughed again and managed to whisper, "Yes Pa, I think so."

I looked around and saw that I had drawn quite a crowd.

"Wait! What about Tucker?" Feeling fearful, I pushed Pa out of my way so I could see back across the river. But Tucker was nowhere to be seen.

Tears stung my eyes as I tried not to cry in front of the men.

"Come on, Little Al. Let's get you to camp so we can get you dried off." Pa said helping me to my bare feet. He put his arm around my waist and almost carried me to camp. My heart ached with the worst ache I had ever known.

CHAPTER ELEVEN

It was all, my fault. Cole didn't need my help; he was just getting the calf's hoof untangled. I was foolish and now I've lost my horse. I thought I was grown and could be counted on as a waddie, a cowboy. How will Pa ever forgive me? The vision of Tucker struggling in the water will forever be in my mind. When I close my eyes, I feel the bones that lay on the river's bottom. That is Tucker's fate, a skull with a body buried deep in the quicksand. Tears sting my eyes as I finish milking Sassy. I hate being a boy. I wish we never came on this drive. Texas wasn't so bad. Me and Ma could'a lived there forever. With my shirt's sleeve I wiped the tears from my face.

I found Ma at the cook pot and handed her the pail of milk. I suppose I should take my place in line for breakfast. I'm not hungry but I don't know what else to do. I had just walked into the middle of camp, before joining the chow line, when two Indians rode in. I froze staring at them. They were riding horses and leading an extra one. The extra horse was covered in mud and in sorry shape. It looked sad and its head hung down so far its nose almost dragged the ground. I suppose they will want to trade that ol' nag for one from our remuda.

One of the Indians came forward on his horse. I recognized him as the one that had received the steer the night of the stampede. He led the spare horse by its reins up to where I stood. I held my breath. When he looked down at me with his black eyes, he slowly made a nod with his head. Then he dropped the reins at my feet. I looked at the poor horse and my breath caught in my throat. I stumbled forward and threw my arms around his neck. "Tucker," I whispered, holding him as tight as I could.

I looked up at the Indian, smiled, and gave a nod. I don't know what the nod meant but hoped it was something good. The Indian smiled, then quickly turned to join his friend. The two of them rode across the river and up the mesa. They were soon out of sight.

"If that don't beat all," I heard someone say.

"I ain't never seen anythang like it." I heard someone else say.

The men began to jaw about the Indians. I didn't listen; I had Tucker to attend to. I led my tired horse over to our wagon and tied him tight. I wasn't going to risk losing him again. The men soon ceased their chatter about the visitors and got back in line for breakfast. I found that I was a little hungry myself.

After a breakfast of biscuits and gravy with sausage, I took a brush and bucket from our wagon and led Tucker down to the river. He wanted nothing to do with the water. He planted his hooves solid into the ground, refusing to go any closer. I dipped the bucket into the river's edge, filling it with water and started the job of scrubbing my horse where he stood.

I hadn't been scrubbing for long when I heard a noise behind me. I turned to find Pa standing there.

"Hey, Pa. Ain't it good that I got Tucker back?" I said while scrubbing.

"Yer one lucky cowboy," he said.

"Yes Pa, I know." He called me cowboy. He must not be too awfully mad. "Why do you think those Indians brought Tucker to me?"

"Only the good Lord knows, Allie Jo. Nothin like that has ever happened before. They must'a taken a shine to ya. That's the only thang I can think of."

"I'm awfully glad of it, Pa. I don't know what I'd do without Tucker. We've had him all my life."

"Life out here can be lost in the blink of an eye," he said looking across the river. "I saw a man drowned in a river like this one once. His horse tossed him and he was bitten by a water moccasin. He might have made it if he hadn't panicked. He had always been afraid of snakes. I couldn't get to him in time and it has always worn heavy on my heart."

"That's sad, Pa. Was he your friend?"

"No." Pa said. Pain showed in his face. "He was my brother." He coughed. "Well I hope you've learned from all this and pay attention to what you should be doin'. Someone may have to count on you one day."

"Yes sir, Pa, I promise I will pay very good attention. I'm so sorry."

Pa patted my back as he went to leave, "I know ya are," he said softly. "Better git that horse cleaned up. We're pullin' out at daybreak tomorrow."

"I will Pa!"

That night as I laid under the wagon looking into the dark evening sky, I starred at the twinkling stars and I thanked the Lord for sparing Tucker's life. I saw a light flickering in the distance; the same as I've seen every night; Cole's campfire. What does he do out there all alone?

CHAPTER TWELVE

Daybreak arrived awfully fast. I milked Sassy, and then ran to get breakfast. My bare feet felt the chill of the cool dirt. I fell in line behind Levi. His red hair glistened in the early morning sun. The men all took baths last night. I stayed at the wagon with Ma. I had my bath while crossing that horrible river. I don't think I need another one just yet.

Breakfast of corn grits and eggs was soon over and everyone had started saddling their horses, including me. I was cinching up Tucker, when someone tapped me on the shoulder. I turned to find Cole standing there. His blond hair clean and shining in the sun. His blue eyes looking down on me, soft and warm.

"I thought you could use these." He said holding a new pair of moccasin boots. "I always keep an extra pair with me. I cut them down some, so maybe they will fit you. You need protection against the cactus thorns."

He held the boots out to me. I took them and was surprised at how soft they were. I never imagined that they would be soft.

"Thank you, but won't you need them?" I asked.

"No. Mine are still good," he said, then mounted his horse and rode away.

I sat on the ground to pull on my new moccasin boots. They felt good the instant I pulled them on. I had just finished tying the top when my brother, Will, walked up.

"Hey! Where'd ya git them boots?" he asked, stopping to gawk.

"Cole gave them to me." I answered proudly.

"Why'd he do that for? He asked looking a bit puzzled. "You best not let Ma see you with them, white girls ain't suppose to wear nothin' from Injuns."

His face was stern and I knew a fight was coming.

"Yeah, well I ain't no white girl, I'm a waddie on this drive," I blurted back rising to my feet.

"So why'd he give 'em to ya? Is he gitten sweet on ya or sumptun?"

"To protect my feet! It's not likely that you'd give me boots, William." I said as snippy as I could.

"I did, too!" he defended. "And you lost them in the river!"

"Oh." I said. I had forgotten that the boots I lost were an old pair of Will's.

"Well maybe, big brother, you ought to go find them for me," I said, then climbed up on my horse and rode off to meet Lum.

I joined Lum in our place at the end of the herd. The beeves hadn't started to move yet.

"I see ya got some protection on yer feet," Lum said eyeballing my new boots.

"Yeah, Cole gave 'em to me," I answered sticking one foot out to admire my gift.

"He's a right nice young feller," is all Lum said.

It wasn't long before the cattle started their march forward. I'm glad to be back on Tucker. I know that one day I will have to let him go, but not today and hopefully not tomorrow. I keep thinking of those Indians. Why didn't they keep Tucker for themselves? Why did they rescue him, if that is what happened? Maybe I don't know as much about 'em as I think I do.

We traveled a few more days before reaching the New Mexico Territory. New Mexico doesn't look much different than Texas. The yucca has lost its flower and the stalks are drying up. I think New Mexico has a few more yucca plants and maybe more mesquite bushes, but other than that, I don't see much change.

CHAPTER THIRTEEN

The sun was already coming up across the prairie when I rolled out from under the wagon. I felt my nose running, and when I raised my hand to my face I found blood. I quickly untied the bandana from my neck and tried to stop the flow. I pinched my nose and tilted my head back. The blood went straight down my throat gagging me until I vomited. It seemed to help though; the blood began to slow some.

Miguel saw my problem. He opened one of his drawers in the chuck box and pulled out a small jar.

"Put dis in yer nose," he said and handed me the jar.

"Thank you." I said, as I unscrewed the lid.

Inside the jar was a creamy salve. I placed my finger in the jar and gently scooped out a small amount. I rubbed it around on the inside of my nostril, then repeated for the other side. The cream was odorless, and it made everything else odorless too. I handed Miguel back his jar.

He pushed the jar back in my hand, "You keep for awhile. Air muy dry here in New Mexico. You git use to it, then no bleed."

"Thank you, sir," I said and placed the jar in my vest pocket as I went to rinse the blood from my bandana.

Breakfast was light. We all grabbed a handful of jerky and went to saddle up. There was no time to cook; Mr. Lewis wants to leave early. It seems that we are running behind schedule. We have only a few days left and we still have many miles to cover.

About mid-day, Pa came riding back and pulled up beside me.

"We got us another river to cross. It's not as big as the Pecos at Horse Head but it's big enough. I thought I would ride across with ya. Just in case ol' Tucker there gets spooked."

"It's okay, Pa. we can cross it," I said.

"I know ya can. But just in case ya need me, I'll be there," he said continuing to ride along.

"Really, Pa, I'm not a baby," I said trying not to sound like I was headed toward a hissy fit.

Pa leaned to the side of his saddle and looked me in the face, "No? Well yer my baby and I'm stayin." He straightened back in his saddle, focused his gaze straight ahead and continued to ride with me.

How awful. Now I have to ride across the river in front of all the men with my Pa holding my hand. Obviously I can live through the river crossings, but I don't see how I can live past this embarrassment. We finally reached the river. Tucker was a little skittish about going in, but he finally did; and I was more nervous than I thought I would be. It did make me feel better knowing Pa was there, but I can't ever tell him that. He would think he'd have to ride with me all the time!

We let the cattle drink while we had our noonday meal. It wasn't much better than breakfast. It was just a tortilla wrapped around cold beans.

I joined Lum out with the cattle. I looked at him trying to guess how old he might be. He's about Pa's age, I reckoned.

"Lum, how long have you known my Pa?" I finally asked.

He thought a bit and said, "Oh, I'd say about twenty years, give 'er take."

"Twenty years? That's a long time. Did you know Pa's brother? The one that drowned?"

"Yeah, Bill." He slung his leg over his saddle horn, "That was a bad day. Yer Pa disappeared for several weeks. He was pretty grief struck."

"When did that happen?" I asked swinging my own leg over my saddle horn.

"Let's see." He thought briefly, "I guess it was just a little while before yer brother Will was born. Yep, it had to be. I believe he named Will after his brother."

"Oh I see. Did you know me and my brothers when we were little?" I asked.

"Not real well." He paused for a bit, thinking back I suppose. "I guess the last time I was out at yer place, you was just a little tike. You were just learnin' to walk, I think."

"So you've known me for a while, then?" I asked, not really knowing what to say.

He smiled, "Yep, that's why yer pa put you with me. He knew yer secret would be safe." He lowered his leg from the saddle horn and clicked his heels to the side of his horse, "Hep, hep, get up there little doggies."

Lum knew all along? Why didn't Pa tell me? Absently, I reached down and adjusted the top of my moccasin boot. I wished Cole knew my secret.

CHAPTER FOURTEEN

We followed the Pecos River until it was joined by the Rio Hondo. There sat a cattle camp where the two rivers come together. The cattle were corralled in the biggest stockyard I had ever seen! Dung heaps were everywhere and so was the smell. I climbed down from my horse and took in the sight of the small settlement. Tents were scattered all about, old and tattered. There was only one building, a wood slab structure that had a sign nailed over the door that simply read–MERCANTILE.

"Here ya are, Little Al. A double Eagle for the hard work ya done out there on the trail. Yer welcome to work for me anytime, that is, when ya get a couple more years on ya and a little more meat on them bones."

The shiny coin tumbled from the trail boss's hand.

"Yes sir!" I smiled. A twenty dollar gold piece, I've never dreamed of making so much money. My thumb slowly rubbed across the liberty head as the man rode off, then I flipped it over to see the magnificent eagle. How wonderful! With this I can buy a new dress and maybe a pair of girl shoes. I can't wait to show Ma.

"Hey kid! Whatcha got there?"

My mind snapped back to the cowboy sitting on his horse. My eyes noticed the familiar moccasin boot, as my eyes made their way up to see Cole smiling down at me.

"It's a twenty-dollar gold piece." I proudly displayed it for him to see.

He leaned down closer to me. His eyes quickly darted about the street. "Ya might not want to show that coin off around here. Ya never know who's watchin'."

His eyes held my attention. Once before I had noticed how soft and friendly they were, when he gave me my new boots. Somehow I felt funny, like my heart hic-cupped or something.

He slowly sat back up on his horse. A soft breeze tousled his blonde hair.

"Whatcha gonna buy with all that money?" he asked.

"I haven't decided yet." Embarrassed, I shoved the coin down into my vest pocket.

"Well, maybe I'll see when we come back through here."

I nodded, "Yeah, well, maybe ya will."

He smiled at me again and then he did the strangest thing... he winked at me.

"See ya, Allie Jo." He flipped the reins on his horse's rump and galloped off to join the other men.

My heart raced as I watched him ride away. Wait! Did he say ALLIE JO?

COMING 2010

TRAIL FROM YESTERDAY

By Carrol Haushalter

When five year old Cole Howard was taken during an Indian raid he not only lost his family but his white heritage. Seven years later, soldiers came, sending his Indian family to the reservation and him back a world he no longer belonged in. Lost between two lives, he turned to cattle driving to outrun the past and maybe find his future.

Carrol Haushalter began earning writing credits with articles in the co-op newspaper in Ponderay, Idaho.

After relocating to Molalla Oregon, she pursued her writing in earnest, creating several children's stories. Her most popular, *Henry Goes to Church,* is a regular feature of the story time she presents with her lead character, Henry, a Nubian goat.

She is a member of the 'Friends of the Molalla Public Library and writes a monthly article on the library for the local newspaper.

Stories of her Great-Grandmother's journey from Texas to New Mexico as part of a cattle drive inspired her to begin to explore the old west through her novel *TRAIL TO TOMORROW.*

To add authenticity to her story, she and her husband joined an actual cattle drive in 2008 with the Burnt Well Guest Ranch owned and operated by Kim and Patricia Chesser in Roswell, New Mexico.

5008567R0

Made in the USA
Charleston, SC
17 April 2010